Anywhere Farm

For Ellen and Van
P. R.

For Sebastian
G. B. K.

First published 2017 by Walker Books Ltd
87 Vauxhall Walk, London SE11 5HJ

2 4 6 8 10 9 7 5 3 1

Text © 2017 Phyllis Root
Illustrations © 2017 G. Brian Karas

This book has been typeset in Clichee and Berlinner Grotesk

Printed in China

British Library Cataloguing in Publication Data:
a catalogue record for this book is available from the British Library

ISBN 978-1-4063-7668-5

www.walker.co.uk

Anywhere Farm

Phyllis Root

illustrated by G. Brian Karas

WALKER BOOKS
AND SUBSIDIARIES
LONDON · BOSTON · SYDNEY · AUCKLAND

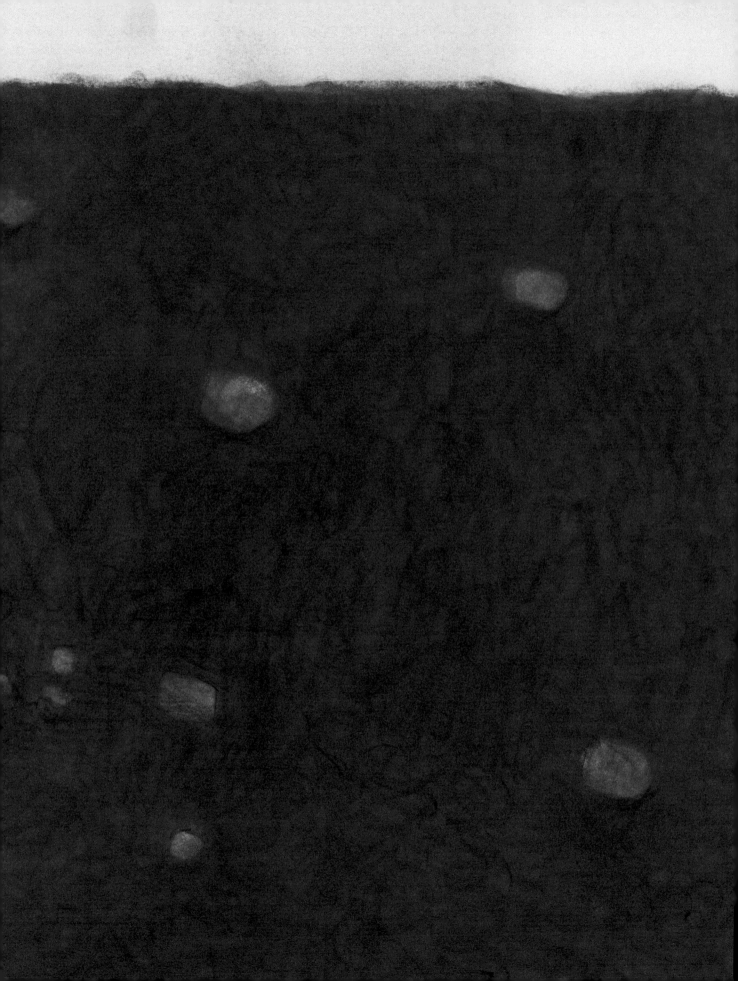

For an anywhere farm, here's all that you need:

 soil

and sunshine,

 some water,

a seed.

Fat seed or skinny seed,
pointy or round,
tenderly tuck it
down into the ground.

Then you watch and you wait.
You water. You weed.
Your seed will sprout out
at its own seedy speed.

And you'll have an anywhere,
anywhere farm.

Where can
you plant
your
anywhere
farm?

An old empty space
makes a good growing place.
But a pan or a bucket,
a pot or a shoe,
a bin or a tin
or a window will do.

Plant a farm in a crate!
Plant a farm in a cup!
In a box on a balcony
ten floors up!

Plant a farm in a truck!

In a box on a bike!

Plant an anywhere farm
anywhere that you like.

Anywhere that you have
some soil, some seed,
some sunshine and water.
(That's all that you need.)

For your

anywhere,

anywhere,

anywhere
farm.

Kale in a pail.

Corn in a horn.

Beets and courgettes,   carrots and broccoli,
oregano, beans,   radishes, greens.

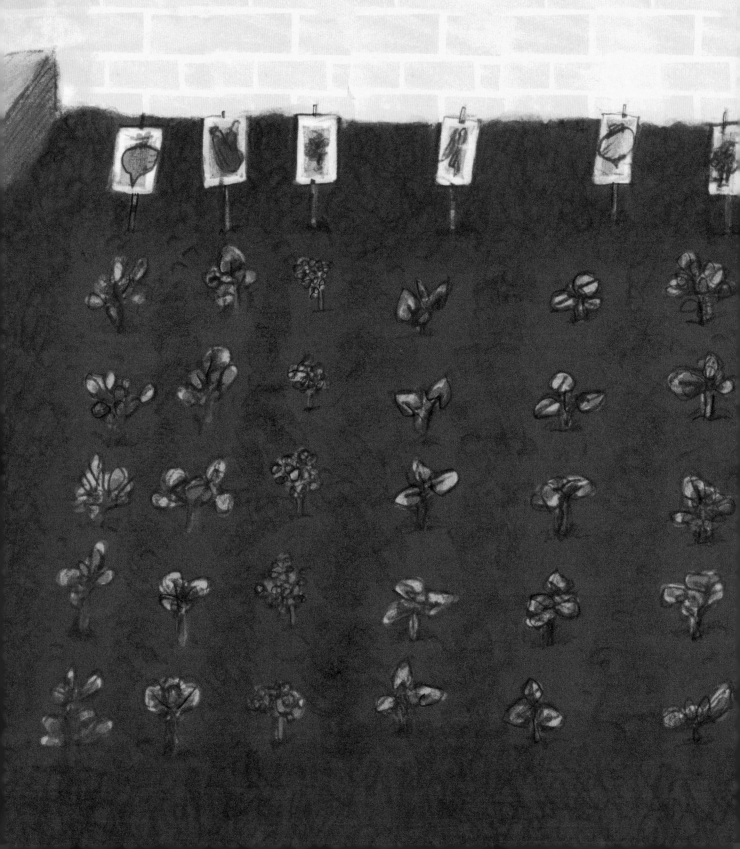

Tomatoes, potatoes,
peppers and peas.

On your anywhere farm,
plant whatever you please.

You might see a butterfly,
ladybirds,
bees,
woodpigeons, beetles,
fat centipedes.

Your neighbours might come.
When they see what you've grown,
they might want an anywhere farm
of their own.

You might give them some seeds
that they plant in a can,
a carton, a bathtub, an old frying pan.

In a boat or a boot
or in their backyard.
Anybody can do it.
You've showed it's not hard.

With your farm in a basket,
and mine on a chair,

with soil and sunshine and water and care,
one day all our anywhere farms anywhere
might turn into ...

an everywhere farm –

everywhere.

Where does it all start?
What do you need?

Just one farmer – you –
and one little seed.